The Country Mouse and the City Mouse

Retold by Alan Benjamin
Illustrated by Jeffrey Severn

For Katie
—A.B.

To Kim and Eric
—J.S.

A GOLDEN BOOK • NEW YORK

Western Publishing Company, Inc., Racine, Wisconsin 53404

Copyright © 1987 by Western Publishing Company, Inc. Illustrations copyright © 1987 by Jeffrey Severn. All rights reserved. Printed in the U.S.A. GOLDEN®, GOLDEN & DESIGN®, and A FIRST LITTLE GOLDEN BOOK® are trademarks of Western Publishing Company, Inc. No part of this book may be reproduced or copied in any form without written permission from the publisher. Library of Congress Catalog Card Number: 86-82425 ISBN: 0-307-10139-8   MCMXCII

A city mouse was once invited to visit a
friend who lived in the country. She had always
been curious about country life, so she packed a
little bag and went merrily on her way.

She found the air fresh and sweet, and the woods and meadows beautiful, carpeted as they were with wildflowers and filled with birdsong.

"This country life is really rather pleasant,"
she thought. But when she sat down to dinner
that evening, she found only some nuts and
berries and a few stalks of wheat on her plate.

"How boring," she moaned to herself, already beginning to feel homesick. She picked at her food, eating just enough so that her friend's feelings would not be hurt.

After dinner, the two went for a walk in the woods. The city mouse told her friend all about her wonderful life in town—about the fine house in which she lived and all the delicious food she enjoyed there. The country mouse was all ears.

It was late when they returned home, and the two settled down for the night. The city mouse had a lot of trouble falling asleep. She was not at all used to the country's night sounds— hooting owls, croaking frogs, and buzzing bugs.

The country mouse, on the other hand, was peacefully dreaming of all the things her friend had told her about life in the city.

At breakfast the next morning, the city mouse found some nuts and berries and a few stalks of wheat on her plate. "Not again," she muttered to herself. "I've had just about enough of this country life.

"How about coming to the city with me for a few days?" the city mouse asked her friend.

"I'd love to," the country mouse replied, and they were soon on their way.

When they arrived at the house in which the city mouse lived, they found the remains of a wonderful dinner on the dining room table. There was roast chicken with all the fixings, a beautiful crumb cake, and a platter of the most delectable cheeses. The country mouse could hardly believe her eyes.

The country mouse had just begun to nibble on a great slab of Swiss cheese when there was a sudden scratching...then a meowing...then a great orange blur!...as the house cat charged into the dining room.

The two mice raced for shelter under the
legs of the tall china cupboard. They stood very
still, barely breathing.

After what seemed like hours, the cat finally left. "Just part of the excitement of city life," said the city mouse with a toss of her whiskers, and the two returned to their interrupted dinner.

The country mouse, still a bit shaken,
helped herself to a tasty morsel of crumb cake.
WHAM! BAM! In marched the boy of the house,
followed by a great shaggy dog!

The two mice fled again, hiding this time in two china mugs. The boy and his dog left as quickly as they'd come, and the house was soon quiet once more.

The country mouse quickly fetched her belongings and spoke to her friend. "My dear, your house is grand indeed, and the food is truly marvelous, but I really prefer the quiet simple life of the country."

The two friends said their farewells and
promised to visit each other again someday.

And perhaps they will.